To Mom
—J.J.

For Carm
—P.O.

Special thanks to Ellen Sands

The Smart Cookie
Text copyright © 2021 by Jory John
Illustrations copyright © 2021 by Pete Oswald
All rights reserved. Made in China.
For information address HarperCollins Children's Books,
a division of HarperCollins Publishers, 195 Broadway, New York, NY 10007.
www.harpercollinschildrens.com

ISBN 978-0-06-304540-8 (trade bdg.) — ISBN 978-0-06-315748-4 (special ed.)
ISBN 978-0-06-320836-0 (intl. ed.)

The artist used scanned watercolor textures
and digital paint to create the illustrations for this book.
22 23 PC 10 9 8 7 6 5 4
❖
First Edition

THE SMART COOKIE

From the #1 *New York Times* Bestselling Team

JORY JOHN AND PETE OSWALD

HARPER

An Imprint of HarperCollinsPublishers

Greetings, I'm a cookie.
I live in a bakery on a street corner near a river.

Come on in!

Welcome to our little community.
It's a warm and supportive place to spend some time.

Pretty fantastic, eh?

These days, life is sweet. But my journey wasn't always a cakewalk.

When I was younger, I couldn't have imagined fitting in here.

For a long time, I didn't feel comfortable speaking up or sharing my ideas. I didn't feel like a *smart* cookie.

I wanted to be a cookie who knew all the answers, a cookie who felt confident in a group, a cookie who said, "AHA!" when solving a puzzle.

Like this:

AHA!

Looking back, I had some trouble in my early days.
I went to school in a gingerbread house.

Our teacher, Ms. Biscotti, was kind and patient.
When I arrived each morning, she'd wave at me
and smile.

But I didn't get the best grades.

And I never raised my hand, because I couldn't think of the answers as fast as the others.

And I was the last to finish most tests.

"Sigh."

It wasn't because I didn't care.
And it wasn't because I didn't try.
Sometimes, I'd get distracted
and mess up, even though
I knew the material.
Those were the most
frustrating moments
of all.

Once, I misspelled
the word "dough."
That was rough!

Another time, I
added when I meant
to *subtract*!

Occasionally, we'd have a lesson where I had absolutely *no idea* what was happening. I just couldn't keep up.

I imagined that my desk was a raft and that I was completely lost at sea. Because that's what

At night, I slept in a cookie jar.
I had about six-dozen roommates.

"Sigh."

I'd stay awake and stare out the window and worry.

And it went this way, day after *day* after *DAY*.

But then *something* happened that changed *everything*.

It all started with a homework assignment.
Ms. Biscotti requested our attention one afternoon.
"Tonight, I would like you to create something completely original," she announced. "It can be anything you want. Please bring it to class tomorrow."

That was it.
There were no further instructions.
Ms. Biscotti winked at me as I gathered my belongings.

I felt like I had a million butterflies in my stomach.

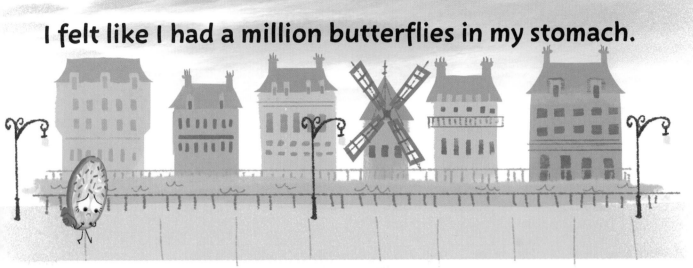

Create *anything*?

Something *original*? Due *tomorrow*?!

Gulp!

When I got home, I immediately went to work.

At first I tried a cooking project. The results were . . . half-baked.

Next I tried to hammer and nail something. It splintered immediately.

Then I tried making a sculpture. It was a complete *bust*! I wondered if I was about to fail yet another assignment. I was stuck.

I stared out the window and watched the rain hit the river. There was something mesmerizing about the water—how it moved in such a chaotic way, swirling around and around, yet ultimately figuring out *exactly* where it needed to go.

AHA!

Suddenly I had an idea. I decided to *write* something original.

A poem!

I came up with a title, based on how I'd been feeling:
"My Crumby Days."
After that, the rest of it seemed to fall into place.

I wrote. And I wrote.

I lost track
of time.

An hour went by in a flash.

AHA!

I said when I was finished.

I couldn't sleep that night.
But it *wasn't* because I was worried.
It was because I was *excited*. I
felt like I had really accomplished
something. I felt . . . *smart*.

The following day, Ms. Biscotti asked for volunteers to share what we'd created.

One kid showed off his original frosting art.

Another kid revealed her sprinkle-distribution machine.

It was neat seeing how everyone was good at such different things.

Finally, Ms. Biscotti turned to me.
"Would *you* like to share anything?" she asked.

"Gulp!" I gulped.
I thought I'd probably
crumble under the
pressure.

But I made my way to the front of the classroom.
I noticed my hands were shaking. My mouth went dry.

"This poem is called 'My Crumby Days,'" I said, my voice cracking. And then I read it aloud.

As I spoke, I noticed some kids nodding at certain lines.

Other kids laughed at parts that were supposed to be funny.

As I built toward the finale, I felt myself becoming more confident and animated.

And, in the end, everybody clapped and cheered!
I promise you this: I'll never, *ever* forget it.

Ms. Biscotti was beaming.
"No one but *you* could've written that poem,"
she said.
"It *was* completely original."

I had *done* it. I'd created something
and shared it with the world.
Well . . . *my* world, at least.